KU-001-529

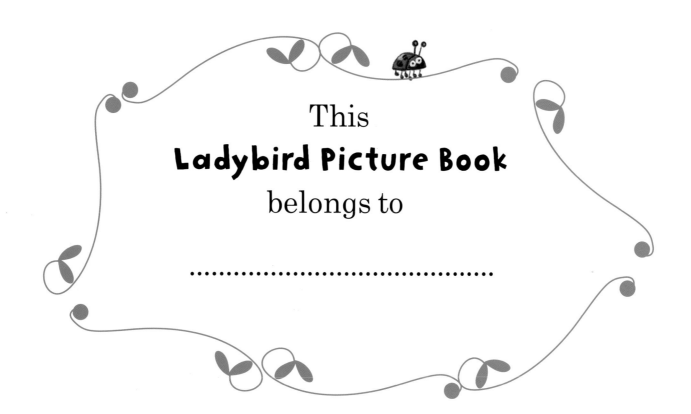

This
Ladybird Picture Book
belongs to

....

LADYBIRD BOOKS

UK | USA | Canada | Ireland | Australia
India | New Zealand | South Africa
Ladybird Books is part of the Penguin Random House group of companies
whose addresses can be found at global.penguinrandomhouse.com.

www.penguin.co.uk   www.puffin.co.uk   www.ladybird.co.uk

First published 1999
Reissued 2014 as part of the Ladybird First Favourite Tales series
This Ladybird Picture Books edition published 2017
001

Copyright © Ladybird Books Ltd, 1999, 2014, 2017

Printed in China
A CIP catalogue record for this book is available from the British Library

ISBN: 978–0–241–31536–1

All correspondence to:
Ladybird Books, Penguin Random House Children's
80 Strand, London WC2R 0RL

Ladybird Picture Books

Chicken Licken

BASED ON A TRADITIONAL FOLK TALE

retold by Mandy Ross ★ illustrated by Sam Childs

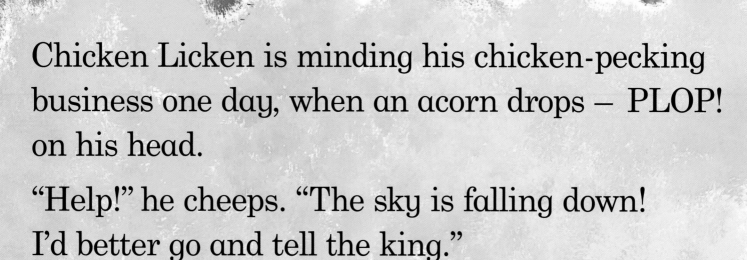

Chicken Licken is minding his chicken-pecking business one day, when an acorn drops – PLOP! on his head.

"Help!" he cheeps. "The sky is falling down! I'd better go and tell the king."

And off he scurries.
"What's the hurry?" clucks...

…Henny Penny.

"Oh, Henny Penny!" cheeps Chicken Licken. "The sky is falling down! I'm off to tell the king."

"That's not funny!" clucks Henny Penny. "I'd better come, too."

And off they scurry.
"What's the hurry?" crows...

We must tell the king.

…Cocky Locky.

"Oh, Cocky Locky!" cheeps Chicken Licken. "The sky is falling down! We're off to tell the king."

"What a cock-a-doodle shock!" crows Cocky Locky. "I'd better come, too."

The king must know!

So Chicken Licken, Henny Penny and Cocky Locky scurry along to tell the king.

"What's the hurry?" quack...

"Oh, Ducky Lucky and Drakey Lakey!" cheeps Chicken Licken. "The sky is falling down! We're off to tell the king."

"You look very shaky!" quacks Drakey Lakey. "We'd better come, too."

So Chicken Licken, Henny Penny, Cocky Locky, Ducky Lucky and Drakey Lakey scurry along to tell the king.

"What's the hurry?" honks ...

…Goosey Loosey.

"Oh, Goosey Loosey!" cheeps Chicken Licken. "The sky is falling down! We're off to tell the king."

"Goodness gracious!" gasps Goosey Loosey. "I'd better come, too."

And off they scurry.
"What's the hurry?" gobbles ...

"Oh, Turkey Lurkey!" cheeps Chicken Licken. "The sky is falling down! We're off to tell the king."

"I feel horribly wobbly," gobbles Turkey Lurkey. "I'd better come, too."

So Chicken Licken, Henny Penny,
Cocky Locky, Ducky Lucky, Drakey Lakey,
Goosey Loosey and Turkey Lurkey scurry
along to tell the king.

This way
to see the
king.

"What's the hurry?" snaps...

"Oh, Foxy Loxy!" cheeps Chicken Licken. "The sky is falling down! We're off to tell the king."

"Aha!" smiles Foxy Loxy. He has a cunning plan.

"Follow me, my feathery friends," smiles Foxy Loxy. "I can help you find the king."

So Chicken Licken, Henny Penny, Cocky Locky, Ducky Lucky, Drakey Lakey, Goosey Loosey and Turkey Lurkey hurry and scurry behind Foxy Loxy, all the way to …

...the Foxy Loxy family lair – just in time for dinner.

And that was the end of Chicken Licken,
Henny Penny, Cocky Locky, Ducky Lucky,
Drakey Lakey, Goosey Loosey and
Turkey Lurkey.

And the king never did find out that the sky
was falling down.

Ladybird Picture Books

Look out for...

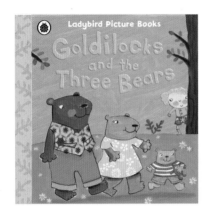

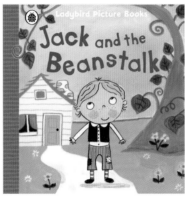

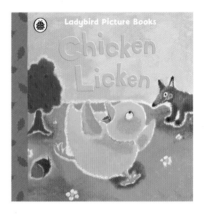

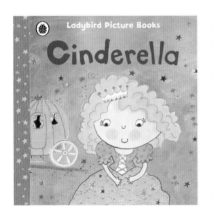

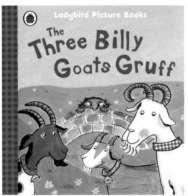

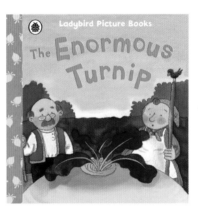

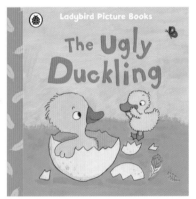

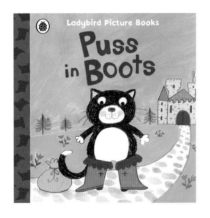